Tickle Your Teacher

Bumper Book of School Jokes

By **Peter Hepplewhite**

Illustrated by **Chambers & Dorsey**

MACMILLAN CHILDREN'S BOOKS

First published 2005 by Macmillan Children's Books
a division of Macmillan Publishers Limited
20 New Wharf Road, London N1 9RR
Basingstoke and Oxford
www.panmacmillan.com

Associated companies throughout the world

ISBN 0 330 43423 3

Text copyright © Peter Hepplewhite 2005
Illustrations copyright © Chambers & Dorsey 2005

The right of Peter Hepplewhite and Chambers & Dorsey to be identified as the
author and illustrator of this work has been asserted by them in accordance
with the Copyright, Designs and Patents Act 1988.

1 3 5 7 9 8 6 4 2

A CIP catalogue record for this book is available from
the British Library.

Typeset by Nigel Hazle
Printed and bound in Great Britain by Mackays of Chatham plc, Kent

For my little jokes, Joe and Andrew

CONTENTS

Tease Your Teacher

Why do surgeons like teachers' hearts for transplants?
They have hardly been used at all!

What do you say when you find a group of teachers up to their necks in wet cement?
'Bring me more cement.'

What's the difference between a teacher and a chimpanzee? Science has proved that chimpanzees can communicate with humans!

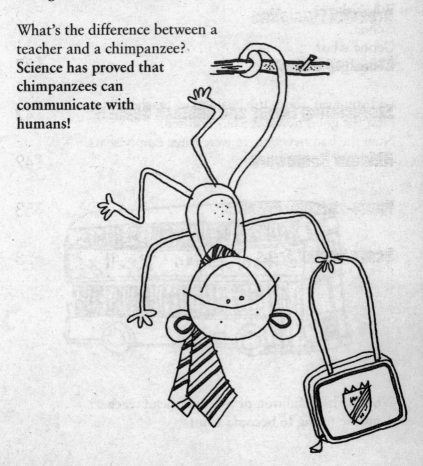

TEACHER: Drone . . . drone . . . bore . . . bore with knobs on . . . JANE! Tommy next to you has fallen asleep. Wake him up!
JANE: **You put him to sleep. You wake him up.**

What do you call a head teacher who is three metres tall and has a potato in each ear?
Anything you like; she can't hear you!

Knock knock.
Who's there?
Genoa.
Genoa who?
Genoa good teacher?

Did you hear about the busload of teachers?
First the good news: the bus crashed.
Now the bad news: there were three empty seats.

What is the definition of a deputy head teacher?
A mouse trying to become a rat!

2

A new teacher was trying to impress his pupils. He stood up in front of the class and said, 'Would everyone who thinks he or she is stupid please stand up.'

After a long silence and a lot of shuffling, a boy got to his feet.

'Well, good morning,' said the teacher. 'So you really think you are a fool?'

The boy answered, 'No, Sir, I just didn't want to see you standing there all by yourself.'

TEACHER: Jane! Wake up! You know you can't sleep in my class.
JANE: I know, Miss. But if you were quieter I'm sure I could.

BOY SQUIRMING IN SEAT: Knock knock, Miss.
TEACHER: Who's there?
BOY: Ahab, Miss.
TEACHER: Ahab who?
BOY: Ahab to go to the toilet. Quick, open the door!

Ten Astounding Ways to Intimidate Your Teacher

(Cut out and arrange in your favourite order of fear)

- >✂

Sit at the front of the classroom and file your teeth into sharp points.

✂- -

When your teacher takes the register and calls your name, yell back:
'Yeah, that's my name. Don't wear it out.'

- >✂

Hold up a large notice that says:
Check the zip on your trousers.

✂- -

Introduce your invisible friend who is sitting beside you. Ask for two copies of all the lesson worksheets.

- >✂

Stick carrots in your ears. Ask your teacher to speak up.

✂- -

Wear a black, hooded cloak to class and shout, 'Unclean.'

Stand up to answer questions and call your teacher 'Your Majesty'.

Shout, 'Great!' or 'Wonderful!' after everything your teacher tells you.

Go to school in your pyjamas and pretend you hadn't noticed.

In a broad Yorkshire accent claim that your name is Albert Higginbottom. If you really are from Yorkshire, insist in an Irish accent that your name is Shaun O'Leprechaun.

There was an old teacher from Jarrow
Whose nose was too long and too narrow
It gave her so much trouble
That she bent it double
And wheeled it round school in a barrow.

There was a young teacher from Leeds
Who swallowed a packet of seeds
In less than an hour
Her left leg was a flower
And her hair was covered in weeds.

Three teachers die and go to heaven. They find themselves at the Pearly Gates, but before they are allowed in St Peter asks them each a question.

'When the children from your class are gathered around your coffin, what would you like them to say about you?'

The first teacher says, 'I would like them to say: "He was a great maths teacher and a very kind man."'

The second teacher says, 'I would like them to say: "He was a wonderful PE teacher. The sun always seemed to shine during his lessons."'

The last teacher replies, 'I would like them to say . . . "CALL AN AMBULANCE. SHE'S MOVING!"'

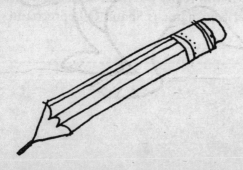

Dear Teacher, we miss you so
Now into hospital you have to go
For you to stay there is a sin
We are very sorry for the banana skin.

NEW TEACHER: What's your name, boy?
BOY: James.
TEACHER: You should say 'Sir'.
JAMES: OK, Sir James.

TEACHER: You drive
me round the bend,
Fred. How can you make
so many mistakes in one
day?
FRED: Because I get here
early, Sir.

What's the difference
between a daft dog
and a short-sighted
teacher?
One barks
madly and
the other
marks
badly!

My teacher talks to herself. Does yours?
Yeah, but she doesn't know it. She thinks we're listening.

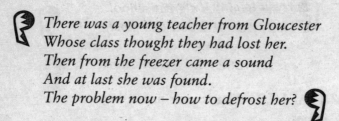

There was a young teacher from Gloucester
Whose class thought they had lost her.
Then from the freezer came a sound
And at last she was found.
The problem now – how to defrost her?

TEACHER: What a cross face! What would you say if I
came to school with a face like that?
PICKED-ON PETER: I'd be too polite to mention it.

What do you call a teacher who keeps a wild ferret down
his trousers?
Very, very stupid!

What do you call a teacher who picks his nose?
The bogeyman!

Head- teacher Trouble

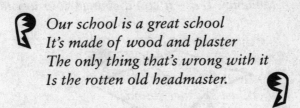

Our school is a great school
It's made of wood and plaster
The only thing that's wrong with it
Is the rotten old headmaster.

Why was the headmaster worried?
Because there were so many rulers in the school!

What is the difference between God and a head teacher?
God knows he is not a head teacher!

Why did the headmaster marry the school cleaner?
She swept him off his feet!

Teacher Test

Are you in danger of turning into a teacher? Take this Teacherish-tendency Test – it could change your whole life.

Do badly behaved children annoy you so much that you just have to tell them off?   YES ☐   NO ☐

Do you talk to everyone as if they were very small children ?   YES ☐   NO ☐

Do you encourage your brothers and sisters by saying things like 'Well done' and 'Aren't you a good little helper?'   YES ☐   NO ☐

Do you tell your parents that they must finish all the housework before they can watch an hour of television?   YES ☐   NO ☐

Do you like very old cars and wouldn't be ashamed to be seen driving one? **YES** ☐ **NO** ☐

Do you like weird ties, elbow patches and brightly coloured checked socks? **YES** ☐ **NO** ☐

Do you know a hundred good reasons for being late? **YES** ☐ **NO** ☐

Do you like bossing your friends into doing what you want ? **YES** ☐ **NO** ☐

Score more than five? Beware, you are showing several disturbing teacherish tendencies!

The Famous Last Words of Terrified Teachers

Is it true that the new girl in Class 3
is a cannibal?

Thank you for the lovely bowl of
wild mushrooms . . .

Hey, that's not a
violin . . .

You wouldn't hit a lady with glasses
on, would you?

I've seen this done on TV . . .

Let me through, boys. I'll deal with
this . . .

OK, I've told you for the last
time . . .

This coffee doesn't taste right . . .

You can't fool me with that old trick. I always tie my shoelaces tightly . . .

Let that down slowly, boys . . .

Who brought that Dobermann to school?

Add your own: _
_ _
_ _
_ _
_ _
_ _ _ _ _ _ _ _ _ _ _ _ _ _ _
_ _ _ _ _ _ _ _ _
_ _ _ _ _ _ _
_ _ _ _ _ _ _ _
_ _ _ _ _ _ _ _

Did you hear about the horrible, hairy teacher who did farmyard impressions?
She didn't just make the noises – she made the SMELLS. PHEWWW!

What did the zombie teacher get his medal for?
Deadication to duty!

What's the difference between a boring teacher and a boring book?
You can shut the book up!

A teacher went to the doctor's one day and said:
'I slipped on a cabbage leaf in the dining room and when I picked myself up I found a terrible thing. If I touched my leg, my arms, my head, my tummy or anything else, it really hurt.'

'Mmmm,' the doctor said. 'I know what the trouble is: You've broken your finger.'

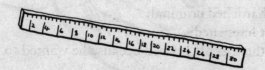

Knock knock.
Who's there?
Clothes on.
Clothes on who?
The school's clothes on Christmas Day. Go away!

What do you get when you cross a computer with a teacher?
A hard driver!

What do you call a teacher
who stops a river?
Adam!

Did you hear about the teacher who became a burglar?
No. What happened?
He fell into a cement mixer on his first break-in and became a hardened criminal.
Then what happened?
He sawed the legs off his bed because he wanted to lie low.

What do you get when you cross a teacher with a vampire?
Lots of blood tests!

There was an old teacher called Peach
Who took his class to the beach
It said on a sign
LOOK OUT FOR THE MINE
The last thing they heard was his screech.

Teacher Strikes Back

TEACHER: Tom, why don't you answer me when I ask you a question?
TOM: I did. I shook my head.
TEACHER: You don't expect me to hear it rattling from here, do you?

What do you get if you cross a teacher with a tiger?
I don't know, but if it was
giving a lesson I'd
really pay
attention.

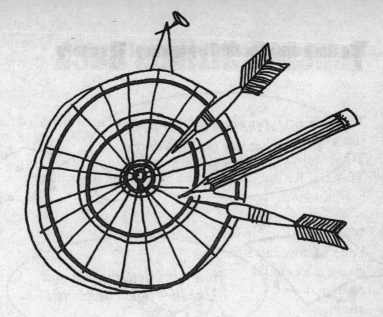

Teacher! Teacher! My head hurts.
Shut up and move away from the dart board!

Why did the teacher put the lights on?
Because the class was so dim!

TEACHER: The human brain is a wonderful thing, boy.
It's a pity yours came from a monkey!

What do say to a teacher armed with a machine-gun.
YES, SIR!!!

Teacher! Teacher! Are you sure this is how you learn to
swim.
Shut up and get back in the sack!

Teacher! Teacher! Why am I running round in circles?
Shut up or I'll nail your other foot to the floor!

Don't Knock About with Your Teacher . . .

Knock knock.
Who's there?
Alex!
Alex who?
Alex the questions
around here!

Knock knock.
Who's there?
Don.
Don who?
Don just stand there, girl, say something!

Knock knock.
Who's there?
Adam.
Adam who?
Adam up and tell me the total!

Knock knock.
Who's there?
Anya.
Anya who?
Anya best behaviour!

Knock knock.
Who's there?
Acid.
Acid who?
Acid down and be quiet!

Knock knock.
Who's there?
D-1.
D-1 who?
D-1 one who is in charge! Now sit down and shut up.

Knock knock.
Who's there?
Thatcher.
Thatcher who?
Thatcher were going to get away with it, did you?

A teacher hurt his back just before he started work at a new school. He went to hospital and had a plaster cast fitted around his upper body – front and back, neck to tum. He was worried about how he would look but delighted to find that his biggest shirt covered all the plaster.

On the first day of term the head teacher gave him his timetable and he was shocked to find he had the roughest and toughest class in school. As he walked up to the classroom he noticed pinned to the door: CLASS 3: WE EAT NEW TEACHERS.

We'll see about that, he thought. Walking confidently into the rowdy classroom, he smiled and flung open the window to let in fresh air. When the breeze made his tie flap about he grabbed the desk stapler and stapled the tie to his chest, right through the shirt and the plaster cast.

In a second the room went quiet. And he had no problems with badly behaved pupils that term.

CONTROLLING A CLASS:
RESPECT
THROUGH
FEAR

THE LITTLE BOOK OF
BIG
PUNISHMENTS

WHAT TO
DO WITH
YOUR EXAM
BRIBES
SENSIBLE INVESTMENTS

24

STRATEGIES!
HOW TO FLATTER
RICH
PARENTS

Using Bright Children
to INCREASE
YOUR Personal
WEALTH

THE INTERNET GUIDE TO CHILD SLAVE
AUCTIONS

Teacher! Teacher! I keep thinking I'm a deck of cards.
Sit down and I'll deal with you later.
And stop shuffling boy!
Oh, and while you are waiting, give me a hand.

End-of-term Songs in the Staffroom

Roses are red
Violets are blue
Teacher is a psycho
And she is coming to get you.

Teachers are sweet and lovely
Headmasters too
All kids stink
And so do you.

Yes YOU, the nosy boy
peering through the window!

Amusing Art

TEACHER: What are you drawing, Durinda?
DURINDA: It's a picture of a horse in a field eating grass.
TEACHER: I can't see any grass. Can you show me where it is?
DURINDA: The horse ate it.
TEACHER: But I can't see the horse either. Where is he?
DURINDA: He went back to his stable. He didn't want to stay in a field where there wasn't any grass.

How many art teachers does it take to change a light bulb? Ten. One to change the bulb and nine to reassure her how good it looks.

Scene: Class Visit to the Art Gallery

ANGRY TEACHER: Why are you hitting that statue, Annie?
AWKWARD ANNIE: The attendant told me to beat it.

What did the painting say to the wall?
First they framed me, then they hung me!

ART TEACHER: What colours would you paint the sun and the wind?
DAFT DORIS: The sun rose and the wind blue.

What did the art teacher say to her boyfriend on Valentine's Day?
I love you with all my art!

A very posh school inspector was touring the art department. She stopped by one piece of work and looked very stern.

'I suppose this picture of a hideous witch is what you call modern art?' she growled.

'No,' replied the art teacher, 'it's what we call a mirror.'

TEACHER: How do you like doing art, Parvez?
PERKY PARVEZ: I like doing nothing better.

Did you hear about the art teacher who died when the girl threw a pot of paint at her?
She died of an art attack!

Why are art teachers never short of money?
Because they can draw cheques!

Why did the art teacher take a pencil to bed?
Because she wanted to draw the curtains!

KID 1: I wish we could sell our art teachers.
KID 2: Why?
KID 1: I read that in auctions Old Masters are fetching big prices.

The Mona Lisa was taken to court for theft!
She was framed!

AWKWARD ANNIE: Look at this picture, Miss. It's all black blobs and yellow splatters. I don't understand what you are painting.
ART TEACHER: I paint what I feel inside me!
AWKWARD ANNIE: Have you tried Alka-seltzer?

Why was the art teacher a vampire?
She liked to draw blood!

What do you call the famous Italian artist who liked to do his paintings sitting on the fridge?
Bottichilli!

Why does the school dentist help out in art lessons?
He likes drawing teeth!

TEACHER, *looking at Julie's artwork*: That's really
unusual, a painting of a bowl of rotten fruit.
JULIE: Yeah, Miss, I'll have to learn to paint faster.

An art teacher had some paintings for sale in a local
gallery. At lunchtime he went to see if any had been sold.
    'I have some good news and some bad news for you,'
the owner of the gallery replied. 'The good news is that a
gentleman asked about your work and wondered if it

would be worth more money after your death. When I told him that I thought it would, he bought all of your paintings.'

'That's marvellous,' smiled the art teacher. 'But what's the bad news.'

'The buyer was your doctor . . .'

Enjoyable English

ANDREW TO HIS FRIENDS:
I've just had the most horrible
time. First I got tuberculosis, then
diarrhoea and just as I was
getting better I got psoriasis.
FRIENDS: Wow, poor you. Are
you OK now? How did you
survive that lot?
ANDREW: I don't know. It was
the worst spelling test I've ever
had.

TEACHER: What is the plural of
mouse?
ANNE: Mice.
TEACHER: Good. Now who can
tell me the plural of baby?
SMART ALEC: Twins!

When is an English teacher like a
judge?
When she hands out long sentences.

TEACHER: I want you to tell me the longest sentence you
can think of?
DOZY DEREK: Life imprisonment!

What was the teacher's pet fly doing in the alphabet soup?
Learning to spell!

TEACHER, TO NEW GIRL: Have you read any Shakespeare?
NEW GIRL: No, Miss.
TEACHER: What have you read, then?
NEW GIRL: Erm . . . red hair, Miss?

SAM: I think my English teacher loves me.
SALLY: Why?
SAM: She keeps putting little kisses by my homework. Just like these: XXXX

What do elves learn at school?
The Elfabet!

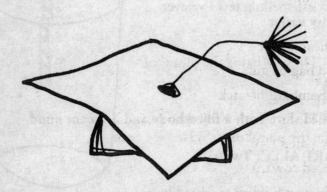

IN-A-HURRY FREDDY: Miss! Miss! I need to go to the toilet.
TEACHER: Again, Freddy? Tell me the alphabet before you go.
FREDDY: A B C D E F G H I J K L M N O Q R S T U V W X Y Z.
TEACHER: Very good, Freddy, but where is the P?
FREDDY: Trickling down my leg, Miss!

Rude Names

Want to call your friends rude names in your English class and get away with it? Use these fine insults and you can truthfully tell your teacher you are just quoting Shakespeare:

serpent's egg

Lapland sorcerer

damnable both sides rogue

monstrous malefactor

ticklebrain

naughty varlet

mad-headed ape

stuffed bag of guts

huge bombard of sack

wretched slave with a filled body and a vacant mind

knotty pated fool

true-bred coward

marble-hearted fool

liege of all loiterers and malcontents

spotted snake with a double tongue

poisonous bunch-backed toad

giant dwarf

you poor worm

fleering tell tale

What is the favourite school subject of young witches and wizards?
Spell-ing!

Why did cavemen draw pictures of hippopotamuses and rhinoceroses on their walls?
Because they couldn't spell them.

Why are the letters O and N important?
Because you can't get on without them!

Text Your Teacher

How do you text a hungry horse in four letters?

M T G G

What letters are bad for your teeth?

D K

What text message frightens away burglars?

I C U

How do you text an order for ham and eggs?

M N X

What letters are bad for your health?

P E

TEACHER: Brian, this essay I asked you to write about milk: it's very short.
BRIEF BRIAN: It's about condensed milk, Miss!

TEACHER: What are you reading, Ravi?
RAVI: Dunno, Miss.
TEACHER: But you're reading out loud!
RAVI: Maybe, but I'm not listening.

TEACHER: An abstract noun is something you can think of but you can't touch. Can someone give me an example, please?
CROSS CHRIS: My dad's new plasma TV.

TEACHER: Who can give me a definition of claustrophobia?
CRAZY CHRIS: An unnatural fear of Santa Claus.

TEACHER: Now listen carefully, class. I want you to construct a sentence using the words: defeat, detail and defence.
FAST FRANKIE: I can, Miss. The cow jumped over defence and detail went over defeat.

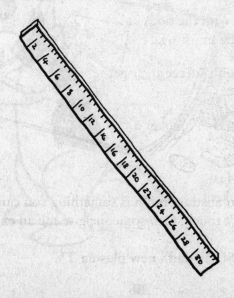

Proverb Pleasure

Look what happened when the teacher asked her class to finish these well-known proverbs . . .

Strike while . . . the fly is near.

A miss is as good as a . . . Mr.

Don't bite the hand that . . . looks grubby.

Never underestimate the power of . . . children.

Never kick a man when he is down . . . he might bite your foot.

There's no fool like . . . the headmaster.

Two's company, three . . . get told off for talking.

If you lie down with the dogs . . . you'll stink in the morning.

If at first you don't succeed . . . get new batteries.

A bird in the hand . . . makes a terrible mess.

He who laughs last . . . didn't get the joke.

TEACHER: Joe, how can you prov
round?
JOE: But, Sir, I never said it was.

Knock knock.
Who's there?
Denial.
Denial who?
Denial's a river in Egypt!

TEACHER
find New
the map,
DICK: T
TEACH
who di
Zealan
LL:

You know, our geography teacher is
showing some parents around the

What is the Capital of France?
F

T
S

TAC
TIMID

TEACH
POSH PA

R: Dick, can you
Zealand on
please.
here it is, Sir.
ER: Now, Jill,
scovered New
d?
Dick did.

s the scariest part of
lia?
Northern Terror-tory!

Why is Europe like a frying pan?
Because it has Greece at the bottom!

CHER: How can we stop polluting our water?
KY SID: Stop taking baths.

HER: What fur do we get from a tiger?
TIM: As fur as possible!

ER: What do we do with crude oil?
ULA: Teach it some manners.

How can you identify crude oil?
It comes out of the ground farting!

A geography teacher on skis,
Went out with a man who said, 'Please,
On the next precipice
Will you give me a kiss?'
She said, 'Quick, before my class sees.'

What do Eskimos use to hold their houses together?
Ig-glue.

TEACHER: Where is the English Channel?
DOZY DEREK: I don't know, my TV doesn't pick it up.

If you travel to Prague, why won't you find any books in
the library?
They are all Czech-ed out!

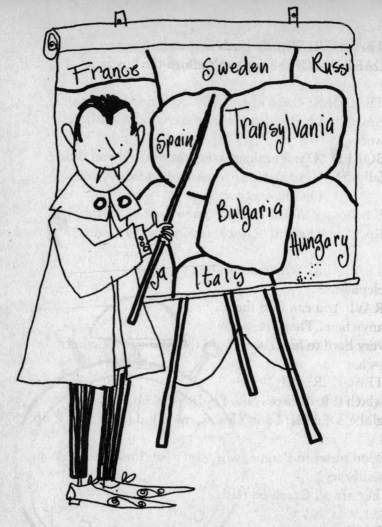

What do you call the small rivers that run into the Nile?
Juve-niles.

TEACHER: What is an American Indian's wife called?
SHARP SHEILA: A Squaw.
TEACHER: Correct! And what are their babies called?
SHEILA: Squawkers!

TEACHER: Why do birds fly south in winter?
DAFT DANNY: They can't afford the bus fare.

TEACHER: Once when I was exploring in South America, I had to live on a tin of ham for a whole week.
BORED BOY: That's amazing, Miss. And you didn't fall off?

Where do geology teachers go in their spare time?
Rock concerts.

TEACHER: Where do we find elephants?
RAVI: You can find them anywhere. They are very hard to hide.

TEACHER: On which side of the globe is Russia?
DIPPY DORA: That's easy, the outside.

What birds are found in Portugal?
Portu-geese.

Quick-fire World Tour

What's the most slippery country in the world?
Greece!

What's the foulest country?
Turkey!

What's the nuttiest country?
Brazil!

What's the coolest country?
Iceland!

Which country has the hottest food?
Chile!

Which country is always starving?
Hungary!

School is fun. Really!

TEACHER: Are you
going to visit Egypt?
ANNA: I Sphinx so.

What is the fussiest sea in
the world?
The Specific Ocean.

TEACHER: What do you call a
boomerang that doesn't work?
BRUCE: A stick!

What do you get from a
pampered cow?
Spoilt milk!

What game do astronauts play?
Moon-opoly!

Hilarious History

What is the difference between a history teacher and a terrorist?
You can negotiate with a terrorist.

Why do Egyptian pyramids have doorbells?
So you can toot-n-come-in.

Who was the biggest thief in history?
Atlas. He held up the whole world.

What was purple and conquered the world?
Alexander the Grape.

What important discovery made Archimedes jump out of his bath and shout, 'Eureka!'?
The water was scalding hot!

Our teacher's an ancient treasure.
We often wonder who dug her up . . .

Our teacher is so old, she remembers when the Dead Sea was just sick!

TEACHER: Who can tell me where Hadrian's Wall is?
SMART ALEC: Round his garden, Miss!

Learn and act out (with sound effects) this awesome (and very long) Roman joke . . .

Set the scene: It is AD 44 – during the Roman invasion of the mysterious island of Britain. A Roman patrol, sent to scout ahead of the main army, comes across a wide river. The soldiers march along until they find a ford. As night closes in, a thick fog swirls over the water.

Suddenly a voice rings out:

'One Celtic warrior is better than any two Roman dumb heads. Cross the river if you dare!'

The outraged centurion sends two of his best men across the ford.

'Bring me the head of that insolent British pig,' he orders. The men wade into the river and are soon hidden by the fog. The sounds of battle echo through the night:

. . . CLANG . . . SMASH . . . AAAARG . . . BANG . . . YERK . . .

Everything goes silent for a few seconds and then a voice yells:

'One Celtic warrior is better than any two Roman dumb heads. Cross the river if you dare!'

This time the centurion is hopping mad. He orders eight of his finest, battle-hardened legionaries to cross the river. They plunge into the fog, screaming for revenge. Again the sounds of battle are heard:

. . . AAAARGH . . .THWACK . . . KERRANG . . . SMASH . . . URGHHH . . .

Then everything goes quiet until a voice yells:

'One Celtic warrior is better than any two Roman dumb heads. Cross the river if you dare!'

By now the centurion is dancing with fury. **'Chop this swine into pieces,'** he orders thirty of his top swordsmen. **'Bring me his head for breakfast.'**

Slowly, deliberately, ready for anything, the squad wades into the river and disappears into the fog. The sounds of battle ring out again:

. . . CLANG . . . DING . . . YERK . . . URGHHH . . . ARRRRGH . . . SMASH . . .

Finally, out of the fog, a lone badly wounded Roman soldier struggles back and collapses in front of the centurion. **'Watch out, it's a trap,'** he moans.

'There's two of them.'

How did the Vikings send secret messages?
In Norse code.

Who invented the first fireplace?
Alfred the Grate.

Why were the early days of history called the Dark Ages?
Because they were full of knights.

What was King Arthur's favourite game?
Knights and crosses!

I wish I had been born a thousand years ago.
Why is that?
Just think of all the history I wouldn't have to learn.

What did the Sheriff of Nottingham say when Robin Hood fired at him?
That was an arrow escape.

TEACHER: Tell me something important that didn't exist one hundred years ago?
ANGUS: Me!

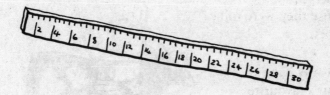

Who invented fractions?
Henry the 1/8.

Why did Henry VIII have so many wives?
He liked to chop and change!

Why was the ghost of Anne Boleyn always running after the ghost of Henry VIII?
She was trying to get ahead!

Where did Napoleon keep his armies?
 Up his sleevies.

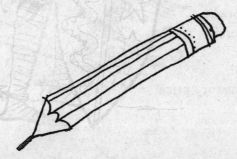

What was Nelson's little brother called?
Half Nelson.

What is Victorian, vicious and lives at the bottom of the sea?
Jack the Kipper.

What kind of lettuce was served on the *Titanic*?
Iceberg!

A Real First World War Joke

OLD LADY TO MAN MILKING COW:
Why aren't you at the front, young man?
MAN: No good, missus. There's no milk at that end.

Knock knock.
Who's there?
Ivan.
Ivan who?
Ivan the history prize!

Heard in playgrounds during the Second World War (to the famous tune from Snow White):

*Whistle while you work
Hitler is a twerp
Goering's barmy
So's his army
Whistle while you work*

What do history teachers do when they go out together?
Make dates.
What do they talk about?
The good old days.

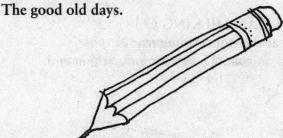

BARRY: I'm learning some ancient history.
LARRY: So am I. Let's go for a walk and talk over old times.

What's the definition of an archaeologist?
A person whose career is in ruins.

The Famous Last Words of Heroic Teachers

*This time machine will
never work . . .*

*Stop playing with that
sword, girl . . .*

*Where did you say you dug up
this bomb, Jenny?*

*What do you mean, Sophie,
you're a reincarnation of Ivan
the Terrible?*

*Listen, class, Sarah's great-
grandfather brought this hand
grenade home during the First
World War . . .*

These castle walls are at least three metres thick. I'll bet they'll stand for another thousand years . . .

Don't worry, the germs in this medieval plague pit will have died hundreds of years ago . . .

Mr Wilkins told me that Class Four have been making gunpowder in science . . .

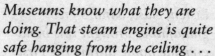

Museums know what they are doing. That steam engine is quite safe hanging from the ceiling . . .

Real Famous Last Words – Honest!

'*Wait till I have finished my problem.*'
Archimedes, the Greek mathematician, was killed in 212 BC. He had helped the city of Syracuse fight the Romans by designing flame-throwers and huge catapults. Archimedes died in the fighting when the city was captured.

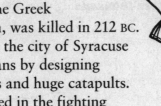

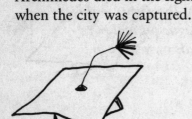

'*Woe is me. I think I am becoming a God.*'
Roman Emperor Vespasian, who died in AD 79.

'*The ladies have to go first . . . Get in the lifeboat, to please me . . . Goodbye, dearie. I'll see you later.*'
John Jacob Astor, the richest man in the world, died on board the 'unsinkable' *Titanic* in 1912.

'*Who is it?*'
Billy the Kid, the American outlaw, was shot by Sheriff Pat Garret at Fort Sumner in 1881.

'*Now I shall go to sleep. Goodnight.*'
Lord Byron, the English poet and hero of
the Greek struggle against the Turks, died
in 1824.

'*They couldn't hit an elephant at
this distance.*'
Union commander General John
Sedgwick died in 1864 during the
American Civil War.

'*All is lost. Monks, monks, monks!*'
King Henry VIII died in 1547.

'*I think I could eat one of Bellamy's
meat pies.*'
The British Prime Minister Pitt the
Younger, who died in 1806.

'*Pardonnez-moi, monsieur.*'
Marie Antoinette, wife of King
Louis XVI of France, was beheaded
in 1793 during the French
Revolution. As she approached the
guillotine, she accidentally stepped
on the foot of her executioner.

It Only Hurts When I Laugh

What do you get when you cross a computer with a banana?
A slipped disk!

Do you turn your computer on with your left hand or your right hand?
Neither, I use the on/off switch.

Why do IT teachers never get sick?
Because an Apple a day keeps the doctor away.

TEACHER: Who can tell me what BC stands for?
SIMPLE SIMON: **Before computers.**

How did the IT teacher get out of prison?
He used the escape key.

Doctor! Doctor! I think I'm part of the Internet.
Well, you do look a site . . .

How does Christopher Robin surf the web?
On the com-pooh-ter.

How do dustmen surf the web?
On the bin-ternet.

How do you make rude noises on the Internet?
With a whoop e-cushion.

How do comedians surf the web?
On the grin-ternet.

How do you surf the web if you are on a diet?
On the thin-ternet.

How do washing machines
surf the web?
On the spin-ternet.

What kind of
ghosts haunt the
Internet?
e-erie ones.

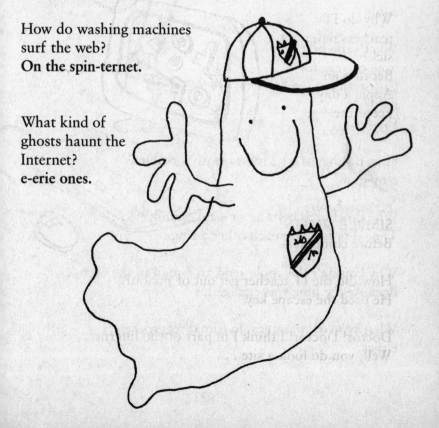

How do you fix a
broken website?
**With stick
e-tape!**

What did Hamlet
say when he was
thinking of sending a
message?
**To e or not to e, that is
the question.**

How do vampires send
mail?
e-vily.

What's the best
time of year for
Christians to send
mail?
E-aster.

How do they start a message in Yorkshire?
e-by-gum.

Why do church bells never send e-mails?
They'd rather give each other a ring.

Why couldn't the apple send an e-mail to the orange?
Because the lime was engaged.

What type of messages do film directors send?
e-pics.

An IT teacher was shipwrecked on her holiday to Silicon Valley. She swam to a small desert island and waited to be rescued. Finally, one day a bottle drifted ashore with a note in it. With shaking hands she pulled it out and read:
Due to lack of use we have regretfully found it necessary to cancel your e-mail account.

IT TEACHER: I think I've got a bug in my computer.
TECHNICIAN: Does the computer make a humming noise?
TEACHER: Yes.
TECHNICIAN: It must be a humbug!

An IT teacher was crossing the road one day when a frog called out to him: 'If you kiss me I'll turn into a beautiful princess.'

He bent down and put the frog into his pocket

With a little croak the frog spoke again: 'If you kiss me I'll turn into a beautiful and very rich princess and reward you handsomely.'

The IT teacher took the frog out of his pocket, smiled fondly at it and put it back again.

Now the frog cried out in a worried voice: 'What's the matter? I've told you I'm a beautiful and very wealthy princess. If you kiss me I'll marry you.'

'Listen,' the IT teacher said, 'my computers are my whole life and I don't have time for girlfriends. But a talking frog . . . that's really cool.'

Things Your IT Teacher Doesn't Want to Hear from You . . .

What back-up?

Are floppy disks really this floppy?

I wonder what happens if I delete this?

So this switch takes down the whole network?

Do you smell something burning?

Sorry. I didn't know that was your directory . . .

Ooops, everyone save your work fast . . .

I think we can plug one more thing into this multi-plug without tripping the breaker . . .

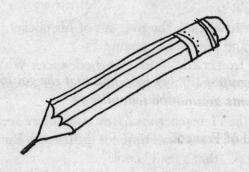

What's that grinding sound?

So it's OK if you drop a hard disk because they're hard, yeah?

The drive won't read this DVD, but fear not – I've got my screwdriver . . .

I didn't know you could do that to a CD!

That DVD drive has eaten my tuna sandwich . . .

Hey, look, everyone! I've discovered the system password . . .

I've heard the latest version of Norton Utilities can't stop this virus . . .

I wonder what this command does . . .

I've never seen it do THAT before!

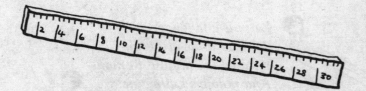

Laughable Languages

How does an Irish potato change its nationality?
It becomes a French fry!

What do French children have for breakfast?
Huit heures bix.

My dad was a Pole.
North or South?

TEACHER: Have you ever seen a duchess?
DOPEY DINAH: Yes, it looks the same as an English 's'.

Knock knock.
Who's there?
Teacher.
Teacher who?
Teach yer-self Spanish!

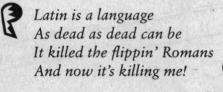

*Latin is a language
As dead as dead can be
It killed the flippin' Romans
And now it's killing me!*

Why did the zombie teach Latin?
Because it was a dead language!

A mummy mouse and a baby mouse are walking along when DANGER . . . they are suddenly attacked by a cat. The mummy mouse jumps in front and yells, 'Grrr! Ruff! Bark!' And the shocked cat runs away.

'You see,' says the mummy mouse to her baby, 'that's why it's important to learn a foreign language.'

What happens when two French pushchairs collide?
They have a crèche!

What's the coldest city in Germany?
Brrr-lin!

Which language is always in a hurry?
Russian! Russian here . . . Russian there.

Which language is the cleanest?
Polish.

What's the best food to try in Paris?
The Trifle Tower!

Where do hamsters come from?
Hamsterdam!

Speak Silly Chinese

I bumped into the table:
Ai Bang Mai Ne

A stupid kid:
Dum Gai

Approach me:
Kum Hia

Great Chinese
invention:
Gun Pao Der

A young
child:
**Ti Ne Bae
Be**

We have reason to believe you are hiding a fugitive:
Hu Yu Hai Ding

Please be quiet:
Wai U Shao Ting

Get Ready for Your Spanish Exchange Visit with this Amazing Joke . . .

Doctor, doctor, me he roto el brazo en varios sitios.
(Doctor, doctor, I have broken my arm in several places.)
Pues yo de usted no volvería a esos sitios.
(Well, if I were you, I wouldn't go back to those places.)

TEACHER: What nationality are you?
NEW KID: Well, my father was born in Iceland and my mother was born in Cuba. So I reckon that makes me an ice cube.

Three foreign-exchange teachers are arguing about which of their languages is the nicest to listen to.

The Spaniard says, 'Just think about the word for "butterfly". In Spanish we pronounce it "Mariposa", a lovely word.'

The Frenchman replies, 'True, but "Papillon", the French word for butterfly, is even more beautiful.'

'And what's the matter with "Schmetterlink"?' asks the German . . .

Pardon My French

Since French cuisine is all the rage
I drink Bored-o with my from-age.
And eat cross-ants with French calf-A.
While wearing a little red beret
So at last I've learned that language fair
And it really makes me deb-an-err.

What do French gangsters fear more than anything else?
The quiche of death!

What do a dog and a bird say when they have dinner?
Bone apa tweet.

Lively Library

Why did the school librarian slip and fall?
Because she was in the non-friction section!

Why didn't the skeleton bring back his overdue book?
Because he was gutless!

How can you tell if an elephant has borrowed a school-library book?
When you open it, peanut shells fall out.

CHEEKY CHARLIE: Do you know how many librarians it takes to change a light bulb?
SCHOOL LIBRARIAN: No, but I'll show you where to look it up!

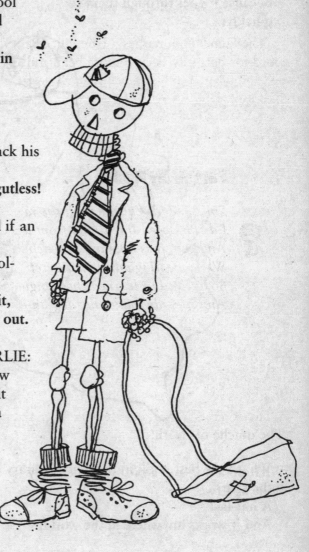

Why does the ghost keep coming
back to the school library for
more books?
**Because it goes through them so
quickly!**

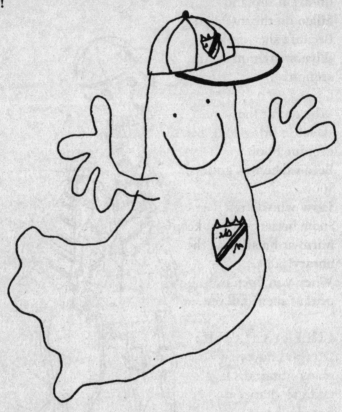

What's the best book in the school library for keeping off
the rain?
A hat-las!
And it works anywhere in the world!

What's the best book to use in the garden?
A dig-tionary!

Why do squirrels sneak into the school
library to use the computers?
To go on the internut!

What was the skeleton
doing in the library?
**Boning up on his favourite
subject.**

Knock knock.
Who's there?
Snow.
Snow who?
Snow better place to keep
warm at break than the
library!

UNLIKELY READING LIST

Great Eggspectations – Charles Chickens

Do You Have a Sixth Sense? – Tel Epath

Make Your Own Fireworks – Dinah Mite

Insect Hunter – Amos Keeto

Winning World War II – Victor Ree

Mountain Climbing – Miles High

Taming Wild Lions – Claude Face

Escaping the Titanic – Mandy Lifeboats

Surviving Winter Storms – S. Keemo

Snowboarding Down Everest – Hugo First

English for Infants – A. B. Cee

The Greatest School Joke Book Ever – J. Ester

More of the Greatest School Humour – J.Okes & J. Apes

How to Be a Magician – M. Erlin

Sewing for Beginners – N. E. Edle & T. H. Read

Make Your Mark in Life — I. Count

Choosing Designer Clothes — Costa Packet

Public Transport in Britain — O. M. Nibus

Learn to Ride — A. Horse

The World's Worst Weather — Gail Storms

Living in Cold Climates — I. C. Places

Great Fish Dishes — D. Oversole

Make Your Own Jewellery — B. Angles & B. Eads

How to Win Games — B. Ingo

Breaking Windows — Eva Stone

Arms and Armour — S. Word & S. Hield

Are You Feeling Lucky? — P. Unk

Coping with Exams — Gladys Over

Great Disasters — Major Blunder

Some Like It Hot — C. Urry

Late Again — Watt Timesit

Self-Defence — G. Ettoff, illustrated by O. R. Else

Great Circus Tricks — B. E. Careful

Ten Years with Santa — Rue Dolf

School Again — Tom Morrow

Five Days at School — Gladys Friday

Training for Head Teachers — E. Vil Ones

Great Holy Places — Cath Edral

Why History Sucks — Anne Guish

Growing Your Own Vegetables — Rosa Cabbages

Knock knock.
Who's there?
Euripedes.
Euripedes who?
Euripedes these books and I'll ban you from the library!

What did one maths book say to the other maths book?
Want to hear my problems?

What did one maths book say to the other maths book
when they had a fight?
Hey, let's stop and work it out!

Why did the knight flick through a book?
He was looking for his page.

What do you call a building with lots of storeys?
The school library.

What does a book do on a cold day?
Put on its jacket!

Mad Maths

TEACHER: If 1 + 1 = 2 and 2 + 2 = 4, what is 7 + 7?
STUCK SUSAN: That's not fair! You answer the easy ones and ask me the hard one!

SON: Dad, will you do my maths homework for me tonight?
DAD: No, son, it wouldn't be right.
SON: Well, at least you could try.

Dim Dorothy was having trouble with adding up.
TEACHER: Now, Dorothy, listen carefully. If you had 10p in one pocket and 10p in another pocket, what would you have?
DIM DOROTHY: Someone else's trousers on!

MATHS TEACHER: If I give you two rabbits and two rabbits and another two rabbits, how many rabbits have you got altogether?

JENNY: Eight!

TEACHER: No, listen again carefully, Jenny. If I give you two rabbits and two rabbits and another two rabbits, how many rabbits have you got?

JENNY: Eight!

TEACHER: We seem to have a problem here. Let's try this. If I give you two oranges and two oranges and another two oranges, how many oranges have you got?

JENNY: Six.

TEACHER: Good girl, Jenny. Now if I give you two rabbits and two rabbits and another two rabbits, how many rabbits have you got altogether?

JENNY: Eight!

TEACHER: How on earth do you work out that three lots of two rabbits is eight?

JENNY: I've already got two pet rabbits at home.

What kind of food do maths teachers eat?
Square meals!

LEE: I'm never going back to that school again!
MUM: Why ever not?
LEE: It's our maths teacher, she's really weird. On Monday she said five and five makes ten. Yesterday she said two and eight makes ten. And today she said four and six makes ten. I'm not going back until she makes up her mind.

TEACHER: Who invented the circle?
ADIL: Sir Cumference.

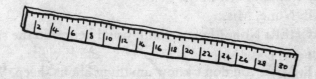

*The new maths
teacher in a country
school was trying to make
her lessons interesting.*

TEACHER: Suppose there were a
dozen sheep and six of them jumped over the fence. How
many would be left in the field?

JANE: None, Miss.

TEACHER: None? Jane, I think you'd better do the sum
again.

**JANE: Miss, you don't know anything about sheep. When
one jumps they all jump!**

TEACHER: If you add 30,412 and 40,273, divide the
answer by 7 and times by 8, what do you get?

PUZZLED PETER: Confused, Sir!

1st ROMAN SOLDIER: What time is it?
2nd ROMAN SOLDIER: XV past III.

TIM: Let's have a race to say our tables.
TOM: *Our tables!* Beat you!

TEACHER: If I had five apples in one hand and six pears in my other hand, what would I have?
IMPRESSED ANISA: Huge hands, Miss!

What kind of tree does a maths teacher climb?
Geometry!

TEACHER: If you had £1 and asked your Dad for another £1, how much would you have?
JIM: £1.
TEACHER: You don't know your sums, Jim!
JIM: You don't know my father, Sir.

What's the longest piece of furniture in the maths room?
The multiplication table!

TEACHER: Why are you so bad at decimals?
TOMMY: I just don't get the point.

What do you call 144 maths teachers?
Gross!

BARRY: Why are you scratching your head?
LARRY: Those maths bugs are biting again.
BARRY: Maths bugs! Never heard of them.
LARRY: Well, some people call them head lice.
BARRY: So why do you call them maths bugs?
LARRY: Because they: add to my misery, take away from my pleasure, divide my attention and multiply like crazy.

TEACHER: If there are seven flies on my desk and I hit one with a ruler, how many are left?
SHARP SUE: Probably just the squidged one!

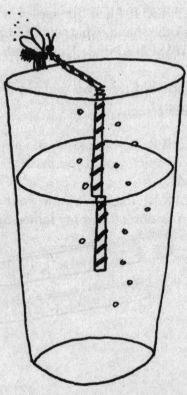

Did you hear what happened when the maths teacher was given a plant by her class?
It grew square roots.

What did the constipated maths teacher do?
Worked it out with a pencil!

There are three kinds of mathematicians – those who can count and those who can't.

What is a kittegory?
A small category!

Why was the month so worried?
Its days were numbered.

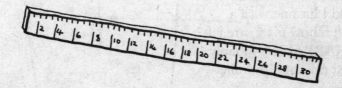

LAZY LARRY: I failed every subject except algebra.
BAFFLED BARRY: Why didn't you fail that?
LARRY: I didn't take it!

TEACHER: If I had 15 marbles in my right trouser pocket, 25 marbles in my left trouser pocket, 20 marbles in my right hip pocket and 30 marbles in my left hip pocket – what would I have?
PUZZLED PATRICK: Heavy trousers, Sir!

Mirthful Music

What's the difference between a girl playing a violin and a dog?
The dog knows when to stop scratching.

A music teacher appears in court. 'Haven't I seen your face before?' demands the judge.

'Yes, Your Honour,' the teacher replies hopefully. 'I gave your son trumpet lessons last spring.'

'Oh yes,' remembered the judge. 'Guilty. Twenty years.'

What do you get when you drop a piano down a mineshaft?
A flat minor.

What do you get when you drop a piano on an army base?
A flat major.

What's the difference between a concert by the school orchestra and World War II? **The concert causes more suffering.**

There was a young girl in the choir
Whose voice got higher and higher
Till one Sunday night
It rose quite out of sight
And they found it next day on the spire.

Why was the piano invented? **So the music teacher had a place to stand his cup of tea.**

What kind of music can you hear in space? **A Nep-tune!**

What musical key do cows sing in? **Beef flat.**

MUSICAL MARY: This tune has been running through my head all day.
TEACHER: **Well there's nothing in there to stop it . . .**

What's the most musical fish
in the sea?
Rock salmon!

MUSIC TEACHER:
What's the French
national anthem
called?
**HUNGRY
HORACE: The
Mayonnaise!**

Why don't skeletons
play music in school?
**They don't have any
organs.**

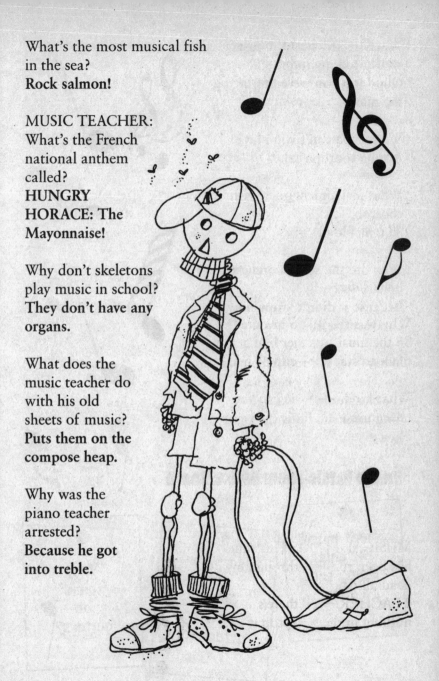

What does the
music teacher do
with his old
sheets of music?
**Puts them on the
compose heap.**

Why was the
piano teacher
arrested?
**Because he got
into treble.**

Teacher! Teacher! I've just swallowed my flute!
Good job you weren't playing the piano.

What tuba can't you play?
A tuba toothpaste!

What instrument goes with cheese?
The pickle-o!

Why did the school orchestra behave so badly?
Because it didn't know how to conduct itself.

What does the music teacher do when she's locked out of the classroom?
Sing until she finds the right key.

On the Music-room Notice Board

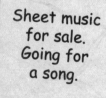

Sheet music for sale. Going for a song.

Harp for sale. Cheap. No strings attached.

Why pick on guitars?

SID: My music teacher is a conductor.
SARISA: Does he conduct the choir or the orchestra?
SID: Electricity, he was struck by lightning.

What has eight feet and can sing?
A quartet!

What was the thief looking for when he broke into the school instrument cupboard?
The lute.

Why is a banana skin in the classroom like music?
Because if you don't C it sharp you'll soon B flat.

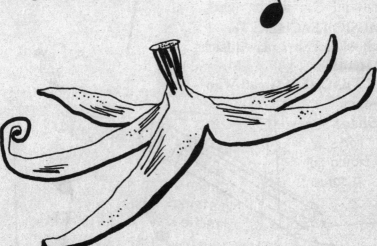

PIANO TEACHER: Your fingers are absolutely filthy!
DIRTY DAN: It's OK, Sir, I'm only using the black keys.

How long did Mozart live?
All his life!

How do you fix a broken tuba?
With a tuba glue!

How do you clean a tuba?
With a tuba toothpaste!

TEACHER: Why have you brought that ladder to the lesson?
KEEN KATIE: You asked me to sing higher.

MUSIC TEACHER: The school orchestra played Bach yesterday . . .
PE TEACHER: Great! Who won?

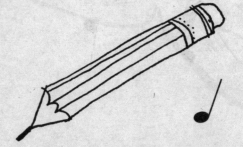

MUSIC TEACHER: Angela, you have a fine voice. Don't spoil it by singing!

Fred, your voice is too good for this world. Save it for the next one!

Ali, you're a natural musician. Your tongue is sharp and your head is flat!

Riotous Religion

Who was the fastest runner in the Bible?
Adam. He was first in the human race.

What kind of lighting did Noah use for the Ark?
Flood lighting!

Did they play tennis in Ancient Egypt?
Yes. The Bible tells how Joseph served in the Pharaoh's court.

The teacher asks her class to draw pictures of their favourite Bible stories. Little Johnny draws four people in an aeroplane.
PUZZLED TEACHER: What's your picture about, Johnny?
JOHNNY: The flight to Egypt, Miss.
TEACHER: I see . . . And that must be Mary, that's Joseph and the small one is baby Jesus. But who is the fourth person?
JOHNNY: That's Pontius – the pilot!

PUPIL: Sir! Sir! Do you know what kind of motor vehicles are in the Bible?

TEACHER: **Don't be silly. They didn't have cars in those days.**

PUPIL: But, Sir. It says David's Triumph was heard throughout the land. And a there must have been a Honda – because the apostles were all in one Accord.

Who was the greatest comedian in the Bible?
Samson. He brought the house down.

Who was the greatest lawbreaker in the Bible?
Moses. He broke all Ten Commandments at once.

How did Adam explain to his children that they no longer lived in the Garden of Eden?
Your mother ate us out of house and home.

What happens when a Buddhist won't stop playing with his computer?
  He enters Nerdvana.

How many Zen Buddhists does it take to change a light bulb?
None. They are the light.

 While shepherds washed their socks by night
All seated round the tub
The Angel of the Lord flew down
And showed them how to scrub.

Why did the school priest giggle?
Mass hysteria.

TEACHER: How did Moses part the Red Sea?
DIPPY DEAN: With a sea-saw!

What do angels dance to at the school disco?
Soul music.

How do RE teachers mark exams?
With spirit levels.

The Atheist and the Monster, Part I

Andy the atheist (a person who doesn't believe in God) was having a quiet day out fishing in Loch Ness when suddenly:
  GRRRR HOOOOWL . . . his boat was attacked by the legendary monster!

  With one toss of its enormous head the monster hurled the boat into the air and opened its mouth wide to swallow him whole.
  As he whirled towards the snapping teeth Andy yelled out: 'Oh, my God! Please help me.'
  At once time froze.
  Andy was trapped in mid-air, looking down the monster's throat.
  Smelling its foul breath.
  Then a booming voice echoed across the Loch:
  'I thought you didn't believe in me?'
  'Come on, God,' Andy begged. 'A minute ago I didn't believe in the Loch Ness Monster either!'

The Atheist and the Monster, Part II

'OK, God, I'm sorry,' said Andy.
'I made a mistake. Please make
this monster religious.'

'So be it,' replied God.

With a crack of thunder, time
unfroze and Andy plunged down
again – towards the monster's
slavering maw.

But this time it politely folded its
claws and prayed:

'Lord, bless this food you have
so graciously sent.'

How does the school
priest get holy water?
Boils the hell out of it!

Favourite Feline Xmas Songs

Have Yourself a Furry Little Xmas

Silent Mice

The First Miaow

Wreck the Halls

Oh Come All Ye Fishful

Long Joke

The RE teacher's cat dies and goes to heaven. God meets him at the Pearly Gates and says, 'You've been a good cat all these years. If there is anything you want, you just have to ask.'

The cat replies, 'Well, I have lived all my life with a poor teacher and had to sleep on hard wooden floors.'

God gets the picture and takes pity on the cat. Shazzam! A fluffy pillow appears and the cat goes to sleep purring contentedly.

A few days later a dozen mice are killed in a tragic accident and go to heaven. God meets them at the Gates with the same kindness he showed the cat.

The mice ask for a special gift. 'All our days,' they explain, 'we have been chased by cats or school caretakers with brooms. If only we had roller skates we wouldn't have to run any more.'

'Your wish is granted,' said God kindly. 'Happy skating.'

A month later God checks up to see how the cat is doing. He is sound asleep on his new pillow, still purring. God wakes him with a tickle and asks:

'How's it going? Are you happy here?'

The cat yawns, stretches and answers: 'It's purrrrfect. I've never been so happy in my life. And those Meals on Wheels you sent round were really tasty.'

SILLY SCIENCE

How can you tell the difference between boys and girls?
Take their genes down.

A science teacher walks into a chemist's shop and asks the pharmacist, 'Do you have any acetylsalicylic acid?'
'You mean aspirin?'
'That's right. I can never remember that word.'

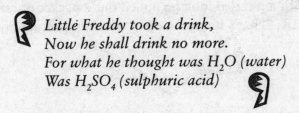

Little Freddy took a drink,
Now he shall drink no more.
For what he thought was H_2O (water)
Was H_2SO_4 (sulphuric acid)

What do you call a boy who can float on water?
Bob.

What part of a fish weighs the most?
The scales.

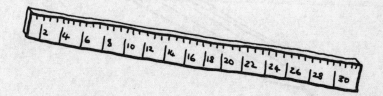

TEACHER: Why are you crying, Ali?
ALI: The lab rats died after I washed them in Persil last night.
TEACHER: You should have known that Persil was bad for rats.
ALI: It wasn't the Persil that killed them. It was the spin dryer.

The science teacher was giving a biology lesson.
TEACHER: 'Now I'll show you the giant cockroach I was keeping in my pocket.'

He put his hand in his pocket and fumbled about for a while. With a puzzled look he pulled out a packet of crisps.
TEACHER: 'That's funny. I clearly remember eating my lunch.'

There was a young teacher named Bright
Who travelled much faster than light
She started one day
In the relative way
And returned on the previous night.

TEACHER: What is the outside of a tree called?
ELLIE: I don't know, Miss.
TEACHER: BARK, Ellie. BARK!
ELLIE: Ruff . . . Grrr . . . Ruff . . . Ruff.

TEACHER: Who can name me the four seasons?
SILLY BILLY: Salt, pepper, mustard and vinegar, Sir.

TEACHER: What is the strongest bird in the world?
SILLIER SALLY: The crane!

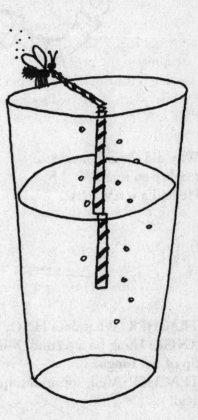

TEACHER: What is the chemical formula for water?
NUTTY NORMAN: H I J K L M N O.
TEACHER: Wrong.
NUTTY NORMAN: How can it be wrong? Yesterday you said the formula for water was H_2O.

What do you get if you eat plutonium?
Atomic ache!

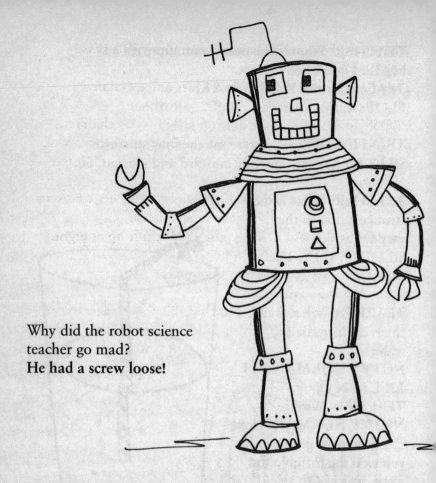

Why did the robot science
teacher go mad?
He had a screw loose!

TEACHER: What does HNO_3 stand for?
**ANISA: Hang on a second, Miss . . . er . . . it's just on the
tip of my tongue . . .**
TEACHER: Well, spit it out, quick. The answer is nitric
acid!

TEACHER: Which is the furthest away, Australia or the
moon?
**DOZY DEREK: Australia, Sir. You can see the moon at
night.**

What does the universe have in common with a sweet shop?
They both have a Milky Way, a Mars and a Galaxy!

CROSS TEACHER: Why did you fall off your chair?
BOUNCING BERYL: I was just demonstrating the law of gravity.

Did you hear about the two dozy science teachers who sent a rocket to the sun without any heat shields?
They thought it was OK because they sent it up at night.

TEACHER: My brain is like a computer.
FRED: What do you mean?
TEACHER: The older I get the less memory it has.

Why did the germ cross the microscope?
To get to the other slide!

What runs but has no legs?
The tap in the science labs!

Why did the science teacher take a ruler to bed?
To see how long he slept.

KEEN KATHY: When I die, I'm going to leave my brain to science.
TEACHER: Well, every little bit helps . . .

The Famous Last Words of Super Science Teachers

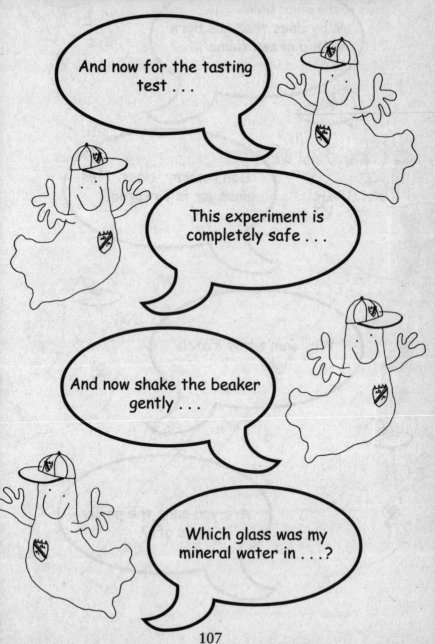

Side-splitting Sport

ALI: I told my PE teacher I was no good at throwing the javelin.
BILLY: What did he say?
ALI: Well, he got the point eventually.

Why couldn't the car play
football?
**It only had one
boot!**

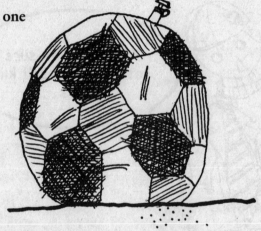

Why did the boy come first in the marathon?
He had athlete's foot!

Why were two flies playing football in a saucer?
They were practising for the cup!

What's the best animal to take to swimming lessons?
The gi-rafft!

What Does PE Stand For?

Physical Exhaustion

Pain Endured

Preferably Evaded

Please Excuse

Produce Extinction

Problem Escaping

Prohibit Enjoyment

Prolonged Evil

Probably Explode

Why was the English cricket
team given lighters?
**Because they kept losing
their matches!**

Why is Ben Nevis
a good listener?
It has so
many
mountain
ears!

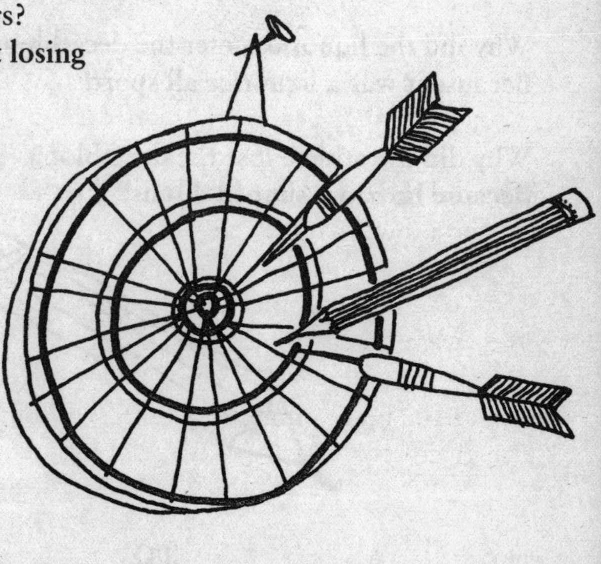

Which school books are best at keeping you fit?
Exercise books!

PE TEACHER: Why didn't you stop that ball?
WEARY WILLIAM: That's what the net is for, isn't it?

What ring is square?
A boxing ring!

Why did the liquorice enter the decathlon?
Because it was a liquorice all sport!

Why did the athlete lose the decathlon?
Because he had a slipped discus!

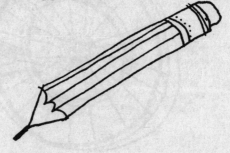

What are the PE teacher's favourite sweets?
Tourna-mints!

Why did the bald PE teacher take up running?
To get some fresh 'air!

A javelin thrower called Vicky
Found the grip of her javelin sticky
When it came to the throw
She couldn't let go
Making judging the distance quite tricky.

How do you start a jelly race?
Get set.

How do you start a teddy
race?
Ready, teddy, go!

What position did
the PE teacher give
the ducks in the
school football
team?
**Left and right
quack!**

Class 6 were out on a walk with their PE teacher. The teacher was trying to make them understand how to read maps and identify the points of the compass.

'If you face north,' she said, 'what's on your right?'

'East,' replied Norman.

'Great,' said the teacher. 'And what's on your left?'

'West,' answered Garry.

'Right again,' said the happy PE teacher. 'And what's behind you?'

'My lunch in my rucksack,' said hungry Hilary.

What is a bee's favourite sport?
Rugbee!

Why didn't the bicycle like sport?
It was too tyred!

Why did the hockey player go to see the vet?
Her calves were hurting!

Why do football players do well in school?
They use their heads!

What's the hardest thing about mountain biking?
When you fall off and hit the ground!

SORROWFUL SAM: Sorry I messed up that goal, Sir. I could kick myself.
PE TEACHER: Don't bother. You'd miss!

PE TEACHER: The national sport in Spain is bullfighting and in England it's cricket.
ANXIOUS ANNIE: I'd rather play cricket.
TEACHER: Why is that?
ANNIE: It's easier to fight crickets.

FRED: We went to the zoo yesterday. Wow, what a trip!
JED: What happened?
FRED: The PE teacher put his head into the lion's mouth to see how many teeth it had.
JED: So?
FRED: The lion closed its mouth to see how many heads the PE teacher had!

PE TEACHER: Why do boxers wear gloves?
DIM DORIS: To stop their hands getting cold!

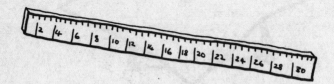

Barmy Breaktimes

Why is the school yard bigger at breaktime?
It has more feet in it!

What did one playground wall say to the other?
Meet you at the corner!

Why did the teacher chase the chickens out of the school yard?
He didn't want to hear any fowl language!

Two boys were fighting in the playground. The teacher was very cross and separated them. She told them off sternly:
  'You mustn't behave like that. You have got to learn to give and take.'
  'Well, Miss,' replied one of the boys, 'he took my sweets and I gave him a thump.'

Why did the jelly baby want to go to school?
Because he wanted to be a Smartie!

What did the horse say when he fell down in the playground?
Help! I can't giddy-up!

HEADMASTER: We are searching the school yard for a boy with a hearing aid.
HELPFUL GIRL: Wouldn't a pair of glasses be more useful?

What do vampire teachers have at 11 o'clock every morning?
A coffin break!

What should the kids do when their teacher hands out rock cakes at break?
Take their pick!

Time Out Tongue Teasers

One-One was a race horse
Two-Two was one too
When One-One won one race
Two-Two won one too.

A fly and a flea in a flue
Were imprisoned, so what could they do?
Said the fly, 'Let us flee!'
'Let us fly!' said the flea.
And they flew through the flaw in the flue.

Irish wristwatch
Irish wristwatch
Irish wristwatch

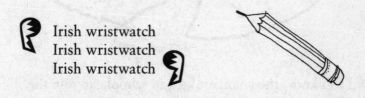

How many cans can a cannibal nibble
If a cannibal can nibble cans?

Why did the teacher drive his car into the school pond?
He was trying to dip his lights!

Where do tadpoles change into frogs?
The croakroom!

Did you know the youngest kids in school can join the army?
No, which part?
The infantry.

What steps would you take if lions attacked your school yard?
Big ones!

All-purpose Rude Rhyme for Boring Breaks

Find out where your favourite teacher comes from and change this verse. It can read Blackpool, Birmingham or Berkshire, in fact anywhere you choose.

My best teacher's from Yorkshire
She's Yorkshire born and bred
She got Yorkshire strength in her arms
And Yorkshire rocks in her head.

TEACHER ON BREAK DUTY: Simon, why are you only wearing one glove? Did you lose one?
SIMPLE SIMON: No, I found one.

TEACHER: Why are you crying, Rosie?
ROSIE: Katie's just broken my new doll.
TEACHER: How did she do that?
ROSIE: When I hit her with it, the head came off.

SCHOOL NURSE: Poor boy. How did you get those dreadful black eyes?
BATTERED BERTIE: See that tree in the playground?
NURSE: Yes.
BERTIE: Well, I didn't.

Written on the Toilet Walls . . .

Don't go to school. Sleep at home.

Don't drink the water. If it can rust iron, think what it's doing to your stomach.

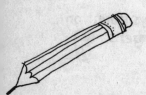

Watch out if you find a wig in the street. It's off its head.

Have you heard the boring joke about the drill?

Our headmaster is SO bald that if he were a tyre he'd be illegal.

Always aim high . . . that way you won't splash your shoes.

There is no future in time travel.

122

Old teachers never die. They just smell bad.

Personal message from the headmaster: I was wrong once —I thought I'd made a mistake!

You can always count on your fingers.

We are the children our parents warned us about!

Cowards rule! If that's OK with you?

I wrote this slowly cos I know you can't read very fast.

Keep smiling. It makes the teachers wonder what you are up to.

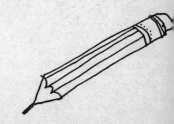

TEACHER: Who gave you that black eye?

BATTLING BRIAN: Nobody gave it to me. I had to fight hard for it!

ANGRY TEACHER: Stupid boy. You nearly knocked me over. Don't you know how to ride your bike yet?

SMART ALEC: 'Yes, it's the bell I can't work.'

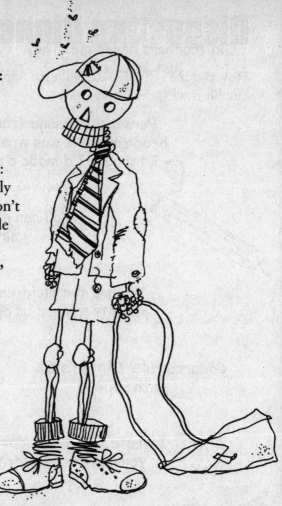

Disgusting Dinners

How did the school cook make an apple crumble?
She hit it with the frying pan!

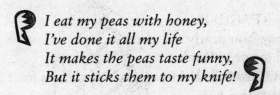

I eat my peas with honey,
I've done it all my life
It makes the peas taste funny,
But it sticks them to my knife!

PUPIL: There's a dead fly in my soup!
DINNER LADY: What do you expect in school dinners? A live one?

What's the place called where they store school dinners?
A mush-room.

DON: How do you think they keep flies out of the school dining room?
JON: Maybe they let them taste the food.

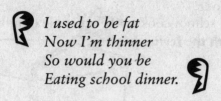

I used to be fat
Now I'm thinner
So would you be
Eating school dinner.

HEAD TEACHER: If I bought 100 iced buns for £1, what would each bun be?
DINNER LADY: Stale.

How did the dinner lady get an electric shock?
She stepped on a fruit scone and the current went up her leg!

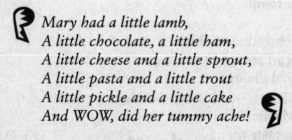

Mary had a little lamb,
A little chocolate, a little ham,
A little cheese and a little sprout,
A little pasta and a little trout
A little pickle and a little cake
And WOW, did her tummy ache!

Why did Daft Danny eat a £1 coin?
His mother told him it was for his school dinner!

What does the dinner lady feed to pixies?
Elf-raising flour!

DINNER LADY: How did you find your sausage, Ramone?
RAMONE: I just moved a chip and there it was!

PUZZLED PERCY: Why is there a button in my salad?
DINNER LADY: It's off the jacket potatoes!

What's yellow, lumpy and stupid?
Thick school custard!

DINNER LADY: Eat up your meat, Horace, it's full of iron.
HUNGRY HORACE: No wonder it's tough.

Have you heard about the school kitchen full of UFOs?
They were unidentified frying objects!

MIFFED MARY: This school food tastes terrible. Bring me the headmaster.
SCHOOL COOK: He won't taste any better.

Menu Board in a School Canteen

OUR LAMB STEAKS TAKE SOME BLEATING

YOU'D BE QUACKERS NOT TO TRY OUR
DUCK STEW

OUR TONGUE SANDWICHES SPEAK
FOR THEMSELVES

OUR CHICKEN SANDWICHES ARE FOWL

OUR TURKEY STICKS TAKE SOME
GOBBLING

TURKEY AND OCTOPUS STEW –
EVERYBODY GETS A LEG

WINSTON: Is the school cook any good?
BORIS: Not really, she burned the salad last week.

What did the tablecloth say to the school dining table?
Don't move, I've got you covered.

IMPATIENT ANNIE: Will the pancakes be long?
DINNER LADY: No, they'll be round as usual.

How can you tell if it's rabbit pie for school dinner?
It has hares in it!

Teacher! Teacher! I keep thinking I'm a strawberry.
Well, sort yourself out before you get in a jam.

TEACHER: Come on, Tim. Eat your cabbage up, it will put colour in your cheeks.
TIM: But, Miss, I don't want green cheeks!

RUDE BOY 1: A crocodile sandwich and make it snappy!

RUDE BOY 2: A frog sandwich. Come on, jump to it!

RUDE BOY 3: A monkey sandwich and don't hang about!

RUDE BOY 4: A cat sandwich and make it purrrfect!

RUDE BOY 5: An egg sandwich – now beat it!

RUDE BOY 6: A lion sandwich – and take some pride in it!

Knock knock.
Who's there?
Egbert.
Egbert who?
Egbert no bacon please!

What happened when the cook mixed egg white with gun powder?
She made a boom-meringue!

What's the difference between roast beef and pea soup?
Nothing. They both taste the same at school. Come to that, so does the custard!

What did the cook's computer do at lunchtime?
Had a byte to eat!

CHEEKY CHARLIE: This school has a really clean canteen.

DINNER LADY: Thank you, Charlie. What makes you say that?

CHARLIE: Everything tastes of soap.

 Humpty Dumpty sat on the wall,
Humpty Dumpty had a great fall,
All the king's horses
And all the king's men
Said, 'Scrambled eggs for dinner again.'

Dreadful Discipline

TEACHER: Ellie, I'd like to go through school for just one day without telling you off!
ELLIE: I wish you would, Miss.

TEACHER: Joseph, I told you to copy this poem out ten times to improve your handwriting and you've only done it six times.
JOSEPH: Looks like my counting isn't up to much either.

Laugh and the class laughs with you.
But you get detention alone!

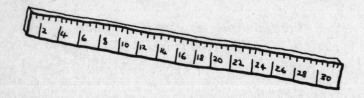

TEACHER: Why are you late, Shaun? Didn't you hear the bell had gone?
SILLY SHAUN: I didn't take it, Sir!

TEACHER: Willy, didn't you hear me call you?
WILLY: Yes, Miss, but yesterday you said not to answer back!

Why did Harry Potter have to leave Hogwarts?
He was ex-spelled!

Been Told off for Calling out in Class? Use One of These Excuses . . .

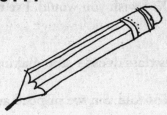

These are new shoes and they are killing me.

I'd been making mud pies at break so I was too embarrassed to put my hand up.

I was an army sergeant in a former life: 'LEFT RIGHT! LEFT RIGHT! HALT.'

Well if you're going to be huffy, next time I'll text you.

At Morning Assembly:

HEAD TEACHER: I have decided to abolish all corporal punishment at this school. That means there will be no physical punishment of any kind.
SHARP SUSAN: So you're stopping school dinners as well?

HEADMISTRESS: Do you think we should allow the older pupils to wear lipstick?
DEPUTY HEAD: Only the girls.

HEADMASTER: Come here, boy! I'll teach you to throw stones at the windows of my room!
NAUGHTY NICK: I wish you would, I've missed ten times.

TEACHER: If this class doesn't stop making a noise, I'm going to go crazy!
RUDE ROGER: Too late, Sir, we stopped an hour ago.

TEACHER: You haven't paid any attention to me this lesson, boy. Are you having trouble hearing?
BORED BORIS: No, Sir, I'm having trouble listening!

TEACHER: Why have you got a banana in each ear?
CHEEKY CHARLENE: Well, Miss, you kept saying that things just went in one ear and out the other . . . so I'm trying to stop them.

TEACHER: Why are you late?
EXHAUSTED EVIE: I slept in.
TEACHER: You mean you sleep at home too?

TEACHER: Class, first the good news! We will only have half a day of school this morning.
CLASS: Hurrah!
TEACHER: And now the bad news. We will have the other half this afternoon.

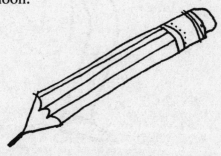

MATHS TEACHER:
I've got a terrible headache. I'm going to get some aspirin and follow the instructions.
MUSIC TEACHER:
What are they?
MATHS TEACHER:
Take two and keep away from children!

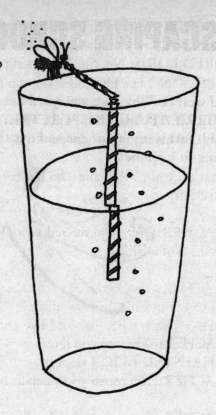

ESCAPING SCHOOL

PUPIL, ON THE PHONE: My son has a deadly disease and won't be able to come to school today!
WORRIED SCHOOL SECRETARY: Who is this speaking?
PUPIL: This is my father speaking . . . oops!

What do you call an ant who hates school?
A tru-ant!

TEACHER: Jane, you missed school yesterday didn't you?
JANE: Not a bit!

TEACHER: You weren't in school last Friday, John. I heard you were out on your bike all day.
JOHN: That's a lie, Sir! And I've got the football tickets in my pocket to prove it.

TEACHER: Nice to see you back at school. How's the broken rib?
DAN: I keep getting a stitch in my side.
TEACHER: Great. That shows the bones are knitting together.

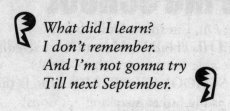

What did I learn?
I don't remember.
And I'm not gonna try
Till next September.

Why did Susie take a hammer to school?
It was breaking-up day!

MOTHER: Come on, Ernest. You have got to get out of bed and go to school.
SON: But, Mum, I don't want to. All the kids hate me, I've got no friends and the teachers pick on me!
MOTHER: Now come on. Enough of this nonsense!
SON: Give me one good reason I've got to go.
MOTHER: You are 44 years old and you are the headmaster!

ALI: You said going to the school dentist would be painless.
TEACHER: **Oh, I'm sorry. Did it hurt?**
ALI: No, but you should have heard him scream when I bit his finger.

Awesome Absence Notes

Annie was absent yesterday because she had a sore trout . . .

Brian will not be in school because he has an acre in his tummy . . .

Please excuse Gail from PE. She fell out of a tree yesterday and has misplaced her hip . . .

My son is under the care of the doctor and shouldn't be taking PE. Please execute him . . .

TEACHER: Why are you late for school again, Chandras?
CHANDRAS: I pulled a muscle in my leg, Miss.
TEACHER: That's a lame excuse!

Mum, will my measles be better next week?
I'm not sure, dear. I hate to make rash promises.

I like going to school. I like going home.
It's the bit in between I don't like.

How is a lion in
the kitchen like a
school on fire?
The sooner you put
it out the better!

140

Excellent Excuses for Being Late for School!

I was at a meeting demanding better pay and conditions for hardworking teachers . . .

My dog swallowed my alarm clock . . .

We have a really old toaster that takes ages to warm up on cold mornings . . .

I was being followed on the way to school by spies, so it took me ten minutes to lose them . . .

My bike ran out of petrol . . .

I'm not late, I'm chronologically challenged . . .

I'm not late. I'm early for tomorrow . . .

My dog went mad and wouldn't let me out of the door . . .

My cat died (three years ago) . . .

My mother had prepared a wonderful breakfast and it would have been an insult to her cooking to rush it . . .

I've discovered I'm allergic to pens and pencils . . .

I helped this little old lady to cross the road and she was really slow . . .

Excrutiating Exams and Rubbish Reports

What's black and white and read all over AND difficult?
An exam paper!

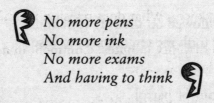 *No more pens*
No more ink
No more exams
And having to think

TEACHER: I hope I didn't see you looking at someone else's exam paper?
FAYAZ: I hope so too, Miss.

What's the best way to pass a geometry test?
Knowing all the angles!

TEACHER: Were you copying Sam's sums?
TOM: No, I was just looking to see if he'd got them right.

How did dinosaurs pass exams?
With extinction!

Annoying Things to Do During a Test – When You Know You Have No Chance of Passing

Twenty minutes into the test, rip up your papers, shout, 'Drat!' and ask for another set.

Come to school in your pyjamas and ask in a dazed voice, 'Is it Monday already?'

Say in a loud voice, 'What does revision mean?'

Walk out after twenty minutes. Comment in a smug voice, 'Well that was easy.'

Make origami animals out of the test papers. Show the moving parts to kids near you.

Sob till you shake, and yell, 'I just can't take it any more.'

Bring in a water pistol.

Dress to suit the test. If it's history, come as a knight. If it's science, wear a white lab coat.

Bring one pencil, break the point and then sharpen it again. Repeat until the test is finished.

Ask a friend to give you a back massage. Tell your teacher it's the latest educational trend and helps your concentration.

Which capital city cheats during tests?
Peking!

ANDY: Have you seen our teacher doing her bird
impressions during tests?
SANDY: Yes. She watches us like a hawk.

Why do teachers like giving tests?
Because they have all the answers!

Which cats score good
marks in tests?
Cheetahs!

Excruciating Exam Errors!

The inhabitants of Ancient Egypt were called mummies . . .

A centurion was a Roman soldier who lived to be 100 . . .

Trees are sometimes planted to break wind . . .

King Arthur lived in the Age of Shivery . . .

Margarine is butter made from fake cows . . .

Sir Francis Drake fought the Spanish Armadillo . . .

Germinate means to become a German citizen . . .

Clouds are high-flying fogs . . .

In some rocks you can find the fossil footprints of fish . . .

A monsoon is a French gentlemen . . .

Wind is like air, only pushier . . .

To stop milk from turning sour – keep it in the cow.

Some people can tell what time it is by looking at the sun. But I can never make out the numbers . . .

King Henry VIII's second wife was called Anne Berlin . . .

Africa is separated from Europe by the sewage canal . . .

DAD: Why have you got such a bad report for history?
SON: Because our stupid teacher keeps asking me about things that happened before I was born.

IAN: My dad's grounded me for getting a terrible report in geography!
ANDREW: That's tough.
IAN: Yeah. How am I supposed to learn more about the world if I can't leave my room?

ZACH: I bite my fingernails before easy exams.
ZEKE: What do you do before a hard exam?
ZACH: I bite other people's fingernails.

My teacher says he gives me tests to find out what I know. But all the questions are about things I don't know!

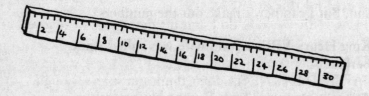

DAUGHTER: Mum, I don't want to go to school today.
MUM: **Why not? Have you got a headache?**
DAUGHTER: No.
MUM: **Have you got a sore throat?**
DAUGHTER: Er, no.
MUM: **Have you got a stomach ache?**
DAUGHTER: No.
MUM: **Well, what have you got?**
DAUGHTER: **A maths test!**

MIFFED MARY: Sir, I really don't think I deserved a mark of zero for this exam.
TEACHER: **Neither do I, but it's the lowest I can give!**

TEACHER: Spell 'Javelin'.
BAFFLED BARNEY: **I don't think I'm sharp enough.**
TEACHER: Try 'knife' then.
BARNEY: **OK, I'll have a stab at it.**

KID 1: I'd rather wrestle with a crocodile than take this history test!
KID 2: You mean there's a choice?

TEACHER: Dan, name two lakes in Switzerland.
DAFT DAN: OK, I'll call them Frederico and Alfonso.

PETER: I didn't know anything before I went to school.
PAULA: I still don't know anything, but now they test me on it!

Hideous Homework

TEACHER: Where is your homework, Angela?
ANGELA: I'm sorry, Miss. I lost it fighting this girl who said you weren't the greatest teacher in the school.

TEACHER: This homework looks like it's in your Dad's handwriting, Thomas.
TRICKY THOMAS: I suppose it's because I used his pen, Sir!

TEACHER: So the dog ate your homework?
PERKY PARVEZ: Yes, Miss.
TEACHER: And where is the dog now?
PARVEZ: At the vets. He doesn't like science any more than I do.

A kid in our class always claimed his dog ate his homework. No one believed him till last week. His dog just graduated from Oxford.

PUPIL: Sir, I didn't do my homework because a brick fell on my head and I lost my memory.
TEACHER: When did this start?
PUPIL: When did what start?

Why did Perfect Peter eat his homework?
The teacher told him it was a piece of cake!

Why shouldn't I write my homework on an empty stomach?
Because paper is much better!

ANGRY TEACHER: How dare you tear your homework into pieces and scatter it round the classroom! What do you think you are doing?
BRAVE BOY: Keeping the werewolves away, Sir!
TEACHER: There are no werewolves!
BOY: Shows it works then, doesn't it?

Ten Terrific Excuses for Not Doing Your Homework
(and the teacher's rude replies)

I fell into a worm hole and woke up in
another universe.
You're always in another world, boy!

My little brother ate it.
Wait 24 hours, then bring me the proof!

My pet hamsters have had babies and
they used it to make a nest.
Bet that knocked the stuffing out of them!

I was abducted by aliens on Friday night
and they kept my homework to study how
the human brain worked.
*If they think your brain is typical, the
Earth is doomed!*

My family are very poor and we had to
burn it to keep warm.
*Would they like the rest of your school
work too?*

I left it in my shirt pocket and my mother
washed it.
*Pity she didn't clean that filthy mind of
yours at the same time!*

The Queen called and she was so impressed by my work she took it home with her.
Why, were the corgis hungry?

Knock knock.
Who's there?
Weevil.
Weevil who?
Weevil work this homework out!

BARRY: I'm going to lead a long life.
SALLY: How do you know?
BARRY: I've got to. It's the only way I'll catch up with all my homework!

TEACHER: I told you to write me a two-page essay about a football match for homework. Why have you only written one line?
JONAH: The game was called off because of bad weather.

KATIE: Mum, we've been doing astronomy at school. And I've got to do my homework on the moon.
MUM: I'm not sure I'm going to let you go!

Panic-stricken Parents

DAD: When I was your age I thought nothing of walking five miles to school, whatever the weather.
CHARLENE: Too right, I don't think much of it myself.

MOTHER: What did you learn in school today?
DAUGHTER: How to write.
MOTHER: Wonderful. What did you write?
DAUGHTER: I don't know, we haven't learned to read yet.

DAD: What did you learn in school today?
SON: Not enough. I have to go back tomorrow.

Letter Sent Home on the First Day of School

Dear Parent,

If you promise not to believe what your child says happens at school, I'll promise not to believe everything he/she says happens at home.

Signed,

A. Wise

Head Teacher

MOTHER: How are you doing in maths?
DAUGHTER: Adding up zeros is no problem, but, hey, those numbers . . . they're tricky!

Mummy! Mummy! Teacher keeps saying I look like a werewolf.
Be quiet, dear, and go and brush your face.

Mummy! Mummy! Teacher keeps saying I look like Frankenstein.
Never mind, dear. Go out and play and don't think about that nasty man. Oh and don't forget to tighten your neck bolts.

MUM: Sally, you've been fighting in school again, haven't you?
SALLY: Yes, Mum.
MUM: You must try and control that hot temper of yours. Didn't I tell you to count to ten?
SALLY: Yes. But Ally's Mum only told her to count to five so she hit me first!

TEACHER: That's the stupidest boy in the whole world!
MOTHER: That's my son!
TEACHER: Oh dear. I am sorry.
MOTHER: You're sorry? Tell me about it!

HEROIC HORACE: A rabid dog tried to eat my school books.
MOTHER: My goodness! What did you do, Horace?
HORACE: I took the words right out of his mouth.

Mum, do you think my school photo does me justice?
With a face like yours, it isn't justice you want, it's mercy.

SINGED SARAH: Mum, I've been banned from science lessons.
MOTHER: Why?
SARAH: Because I blew something up.
MOTHER: What?
SARAH: The science labs.

MUM: How do you like your new teacher?
LITTLE LOTTIE: I don't. She told me to sit down at the front for the present, then she didn't give me one.

EXCITED DAD: What position are you in the school football team, son?
SON: The PE teacher says I'm the main drawback.

DAD: I know you are worried about your exams but you must get some sleep. Do what I do, count sheep.
TIRED TIM: I tried that but by the time I got to 250,317 it was time to get up.

SKIVING SID: I can't go to school today.
DAD: Why not?
SID: I don't feel well.
DAD: Where don't you feel well?
SID: At school.

DAD: Why did you get such a low mark in your history test?
DESPERATE DAN: Absence.
DAD: But you weren't absent on the day of the test.
DAN: No, but the boy who sits next to me was.

GERTIE: Dad, why did God give Moses the tablets?
DREARY DAD: Because he had a headache.

MUM: It's only two days since the summer holidays and your teacher has phoned to complain about your behaviour!
TOM: What did you say?
MUM: I've just had him at home for six weeks and I never called you once when he wouldn't behave.

Scary School Trips

What do you call a flea on a school trip?
An itch hiker!

Teacher! Teacher! I don't want to go to France.
Shut up and keep swimming!

Why did the school bus have a puncture?
Because of the fork in the road!

Class 3 went to France last week. What a week it was. It only rained twice – once for four days and once for three days.

TEACHER: Well, here we are on the Channel ferry, children. And what do we do if a pupil falls into the sea.
HELPFUL HARRY: Yell, 'Pupil overboard,' Miss.
TEACHER: And what do we do if a teacher falls overboard?
HARRY: Depends which teacher, Miss.

DAD: Did you enjoy your school trip to the zoo, son?
DIZZY DOM: It was OK, but a monkey bit my finger.
DAD: Oh dear, which one?
DOM: Dunno, all monkeys look alike to me.

Mum, I need a ladder for school?
Why?
Our teacher said we were going on a climbing holiday.

What do you call a camping ground for spiders?
A website!

FRED: Wow! Did you see that bee just get splatted on the coach windscreen. I wonder what was the last thing was to go through its mind?
JED: Its feet!

Scene: A School Trip to a Farm.

TEACHER: What's the matter? Why are you lying down inside?
LAZY LULU: Well, if I don't see anything, I won't have to write about it.

Scene: Skiing Trip

TEACHER: Right, class, listen carefully. It's very cold outside and you must be sure to wrap up warmly. Last year there was one boy who was so eager to go outside and play with his snowboard that he didn't put a coat or scarf on. He caught a chill and had to be flown home with pneumonia.

CARING CHRIS: What happened to the snowboard?

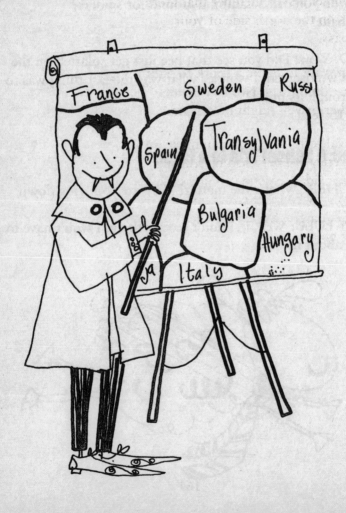

School Camping Trip: Helpful Hints

The fluff from your belly button makes a handy fire starter.

Always wear a long-sleeved shirt. It gives you something to wipe your nose on.

If you get lost, remember that moss grows on the north side of your compass.

If you want to make a spark to light a fire – do not rub two boy Scouts together or you might be arrested.

Survival technique: you can make an emergency sleeping bag by stuffing ducks inside a plastic rubbish sack. **Warning: when you crawl inside don't squash the ducks or they might go quackers.**

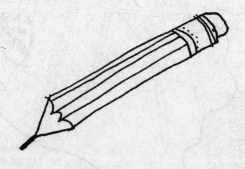

Class 6 were on a flight to Spain. Everyone behaved well except Archie.

He hit the boy next to him . . .

Ran up and down the aisle . . .

Knocked the meals trolley over . . .

And kicked the stewardess . . .

The teacher told Archie off several times but it made no difference.

She stood up and tried to push him into his seat but he pushed her back . . .

Suddenly from the rear of the plane an elderly man walked slowly down the aisle.

He wore the uniform of an RAF Air Marshal and gently asked the flustered teacher to stand aside.

He bent down to talk to Archie, his hand pointing to the medals on his chest. Then the Air Marshal whispered in Archie's ear and instantly the boy calmed down. He sheepishly went over to his teacher and asked if he could sit beside her.

The other passengers burst into

applause and the teacher smiled with relief. As the Air Marshal went back to his seat she asked, 'Excuse me, Sir, but could I ask what you said to Archie? It's had a wonderful effect on him.'

'Certainly,' replied the Air Marshal. 'I showed him my pilot's wings, service stars and campaign ribbons and explained that they give me the right to throw one passenger out of the plane door on any flight I choose.'

Knock knock.
Who's there?
Oooze.
Oooze who?
Oooze in charge of these horrible kids?

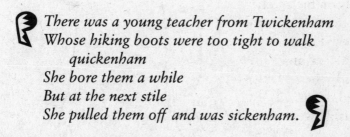

There was a young teacher from Twickenham
Whose hiking boots were too tight to walk
      quickenham
She bore them a while
But at the next stile
She pulled them off and was sickenham.

What's the worst school trip?
The trip to the headmaster's office!

SANDY RANSFORD

1001
Very Funny
Jokes

Be the envy of your friends with this collection of truly side-splitting jokes!

What kind of monster has the best hearing?
The eeriest.

What do athletes do when they're not running?
Surf the sprinternet.

What kind of shoes can you make
out of two banana skins?
A pair of slippers.

What kind of ghost works for the police force?
An in-spectre.

SANDY RANSFORD

Revolting Jokes

**A riot of really revolting jokes
that'll make you go 'yuck!'**

What do executioners write in December?
Their Christmas chopping lists.

Why did the cannibal join the police force?
So he could grill his suspects.

First Flea: You don't look well.
Second Flea: No, I'm not feeling up to scratch.

Where's the best place to have the school sickroom?
Next to the canteen!

A selected list of titles available from
Macmillan Children's Books

The prices shown below are correct at the time of going to press. However, Macmillan Publishers reserves the right to show new retail prices on covers which may differ from those previously advertised.

1001 Very Funny Jokes
    by Sandy Ransford   0 330 42035 6   £3.99

Revolting Jokes
    by Sandy Ransford   0 330 39773 7   £3.99

A Joke for Every Day of the Year
    by Sandy Ransford   0 330 48351 X   £4.99

All Pan Macmillan titles can be ordered from our website, www.panmacmillan.com, or from your local bookshop and are also available by post from:

**Bookpost,
PO Box 29, Douglas, Isle of Man IM99 1BQ**

Credit cards accepted. For details:
Telephone: 01624 677237
Fax: 01624 670923
Email: bookshop@enterprise.net
www.bookpost.co.uk

Free postage and packing in the United Kingdom